Never, EVER Shout in a Zoo

Never, EVER Shout in a Zoo

by Karma Wilson   Illustrated by Doug Cushman

LITTLE, BROWN AND COMPANY
New York ✧ An AOL Time Warner Company

Text copyright © 2004 by Karma Wilson
Illustrations copyright © 2004 by Doug Cushman

First Edition

Library of Congress Cataloging-in-Publication Data

Wilson, Karma.
    Never, ever shout in a zoo / by Karma Wilson ; pictures by Doug Cushman. — 1st ed.
        p. cm.
    Summary: Rhyming text depicts the chaos caused by shouting at the zoo.
    ISBN 0-316-98564-3
    [1. Zoos—Fiction. 2. Zoo animals—Fiction. 3. Stories in rhyme.] I. Cushman, Doug, ill. II. Title.

PZ8.3.W6976Ne 2004
[E]—dc21   2003040270

10 9 8 7 6 5 4 3 2 1

Book design by Alyssa Morris

TWP

Printed in Singapore

The illustrations in this book were done in watercolor and colored pencil on Saunders Waterford Watercolor paper. The text was set in Birdslegs, and the display type is Fontesque.

To my father-in-law, Mike Wilson, who loves animals,
including his rambunctious grandkids. His house turns
into a zoo each time they come for a visit.

—K.W.

For Kelsey and all the animals she's loved.

—D.C.

Never, EVER shout in a zoo . . .
because if you do . . .
anything might happen.
And don't say I didn't warn you.

If you shout in the zoo, you might scare a bear.

A GIANT bear.

A GIANT, GROUCHY bear.

A GIANT, GROUCHY, GRIZZLY bear that weighs two thousand twenty-three pounds!

And if you scare that bear, he just might charge.
A large charge.
A large barge of charge...
right through the bars of his cage!

Uh-oh! Don't say I didn't warn you.

And if that bear gets loose, he might charge past a moose.
A BIG moose.
A BIG BULL moose.
A BIG BULL moose with a bad attitude!

And if that moose sees a bear running loose...
he might get an idea.
A DREADFUL idea.
A DREADFUL, DISASTROUS idea...
that he should be free like that bear.

Uh-oh! Don't say I didn't warn you.

And if the moose escapes, he might trot by the apes!

All . . . those . . . apes.

All those CLEVER apes.

All those CLEVER, CONNIVING apes that love to play practical jokes!

And if those apes should happen to spy
the moose and the bear as they clatter on by...
they might come up with a plan!
A MALICIOUS plan.
A MALICIOUS, MISCHIEVOUS plan to break out like the moose and the bear
and set animals loose EVERYWHERE!

Uh-oh! Don't say I didn't warn you!

And if those apes could do as they please,
they'd probably steal the zookeeper's keys.

They'd let out the hippos!
They'd unleash the lions!
They'd set free the tigers and the kangaroos,
the snakes, the flamingos, the crocodiles...
and EVERY single beast in the zoo!

UH-OH! DON'T SAY I DIDN'T WARN YOU!

All those creatures would scatter about. All because of a shout.
One shout.
One innocent, little shout.

One innocent, little shout that...
STARTED THE WHOLE MESS!

And all those animals running wild might lock up
each man and woman and child at the zoo...
including YOU!

I *warned* you. You can't say I didn't.

And there you would be in a pen. Then . . .
what would you do to get out?
You'd probably shout.
But haven't I warned you?

NEVER, **EVER** SHOUT
IN A ZOO!

New Exhibit!
Dinosaur
frozen in
ICE
from the
ARCTIC!